Bugg

The exterminator s...
wall, looking for more r...

He saw them. Unflinchingly they stared back at him.

They saw him stagger backward, dropping his sprayer. They saw him clutch at his chest, then collapse against a wall.

Through a haze of agony he saw their feelers waving gently in the air. It was as if they were waving good-bye.

That was the last thing he ever saw. Ever.

His body lay still as the roaches came down out of the walls and crawled all over him.

Other X-Files books

Voyager

THE ⊗ FILES™

DIE, BUG, DIE!

A novel by Les Martin

Based on the television series
The X-Files created by
Chris Carter

Based on the teleplay
written by Darin Morgan

HarperCollins*Publishers*

Voyager
An Imprint of HarperCollins*Publishers*
77–85 Fulham Palace Road,
Hammersmith, London W6 8JB

Special overseas edition 1997
First paperback edition 1997
1 2 3 4 5 6 7 8 9

First published in the USA by HarperTrophy
A division of HarperCollins*Publishers* 1997

ISBN 0 00 648312 7

Set in Century

Printed and bound in Great Britain by
Caledonian International Book Manufacturing Ltd, Glasgow

In memory of Brett,
the fabulous feline

Chapter ONE

The man stared at the cockroach.

The cockroach stared back—and started to race for cover.

The man was too fast. His hand shot out and grabbed the cockroach scampering up the cement basement wall.

The man held the roach up, keeping it between his thumb and index finger. It fluttered its antennas helplessly in the air.

"Behold the mighty cockroach," the man said. He sounded like a teacher fondly explaining his favorite subject. He looked like a teacher, too, with a white shirt and a thin black tie, dark slacks, and shiny black shoes. On the back of his shirt, though, was a picture of a roach. Beneath the cartoon, bright red letters spelled DR. BUGGER—EXTERMINATOR. Dr. Bugger cured households of pests, and he loved his work.

"Cockroaches have lived on Earth far longer than we humans," Dr. Bugger informed the man who had hired him, Jeff Eckerle. Eckerle called himself a doctor, too, though the only thing he tried to heal was the environment. He was working to produce nonpolluting artificial fuel. He was a whiz in the lab. But right now, as he stared bug-eyed at the roach in Dr. Bugger's hand, what he was, was nervous.

"Scientists believe that roaches date from three hundred fifty million years ago," Dr. Bugger went on. "Today they can be found all over the world—from the tropics to the Arctic. There are over four thousand known varieties of them, and their numbers keep growing. In a year, a single female can produce over half a million offspring."

Dr. Bugger gazed affectionately at the roach wiggling desperately in his grip. Then he continued, "Nothing can get rid of them completely. They adapt to one poison after another. Even radiation does not kill them. In terms of survival, they are nearly perfect creatures. But of course, that is all they are—simple creatures. They can seek food. They can flee danger. But unlike humans, they cannot think."

"Thank goodness for that," said Dr. Eckerle. His light blue eyes were fixed on the roach. His pale face was even paler than usual.

"Yes," said Dr. Bugger. "Compared to roaches we are like gods. And we can act like gods as well."

With that, Dr. Bugger dropped the roach on the concrete floor. Before it could make a move, Dr.

Bugger stomped it. At the crunching of its shell Dr. Eckerle winced, disgusted.

"Yuck," he said, gazing down at the remains. "You sure it's dead?"

"As a doornail," Dr. Bugger assured him.

"I've heard that even if you chop off their heads, they keep living," Dr. Eckerle said, still jittery. "It just takes them time to die of starvation."

Dr. Bugger shrugged. "Look, buddy, I don't know about that weird stuff. I just kill 'em."

"That's why I hired you," Dr. Eckerle said, still gazing squeamishly at the crushed roach.

"Then watch me go to work," Dr. Bugger said. "We'll be done in no time at all."

Dr. Bugger stooped over and picked up a spray tank. He started spraying the pesticide into cracks in the wall.

"I thought nowadays you froze the bugs to death," Dr. Eckerle said.

"Freeze them? Where's the fun in that?" Dr. Bugger asked. "Now we have a chemical that grows like a fungus. It not only gets rid of the roach that touches it but spreads to any other roach the first roach comes in contact with. This way, the bugs do all the work."

"Just as long as they disappear," Dr. Eckerle said. "If you don't mind, I think I'll skip the show.

Bugs drive me crazy." With a shudder, he headed up the stairs.

The exterminator was grinning as he got down to work. Suddenly his smile vanished. He scowled at a roach on the wall in front of his face. The roach didn't make a move to run away. It actually seemed to be looking at Dr. Bugger defiantly, daring him to try to kill it.

"Why, you arrogant little—" Dr. Bugger snarled, and let loose a squirt of spray. It hit right on target.

The bug didn't lose its grip on the wall. In fact, it didn't seemed harmed at all. It did seem annoyed, though. At least the sharp chirp it made didn't sound very happy.

"I'm gonna have to find a new spray, I guess," Dr. Bugger muttered. "Until then . . ."

With the metal tip of his sprayer he knocked the roach off the wall, then brought his shoe down on top of it.

"When all else fails, nothing beats direct action," he said. Then he lifted his foot, and his mouth dropped open.

He watched as the bug scampered away unscathed.

"Oh, no you don't," Dr. Bugger said, and, moving full speed, chased it down before it could reach cover.

This time he stomped it with all his force.

"Ow!" he cried. It felt as if a nail had gone through the sole of his shoe. He was half blind with pain. Grimacing, he tried to shake it off. He tried to go back to work. He squinted at chinks in the wall, looking for more roaches.

He saw them. Unflinchingly they stared back at him, just the way the last one had.

They saw him stagger backward, dropping his sprayer. They saw him clutch at his chest, then collapse against a wall.

Through a haze of agony Dr. Bugger saw their feelers waving gently in the air. It was as if they were waving good-bye.

That was the last thing Dr. Bugger saw. Ever.

His body lay still as the roaches came down out of the walls and crawled all over him.

It didn't disturb the roaches in the least when Dr. Eckerle came down the stairs saying, "Oh, I forgot to tell you I also found a roach in the—"

They did not even react when he started screaming.

Chapter TWO

FBI Special Agent Fox Mulder was sitting alone in his car, looking up through the windshield at the night sky. He was parked on a New England country road. The night was clear, with no pollution. Bright stars filled the sky. Some stood apart. Others formed glowing clusters. It was an amazing light show. Mulder loved it.

Suddenly Mulder grimaced.

A small black blob landed on his windshield, bringing his thoughts back to earth. Another blob appeared nearby. Then another. Mulder squinted at the glass.

"Bugs," he muttered, and turned on his windshield wipers.

His thoughts were interrupted again as the cellular phone in his pocket chirped.

Annoyed at being dragged away from the splendor of the night sky, Mulder turned off the wipers and picked up the phone.

His partner at the FBI, Special Agent Dana Scully, was on the line.

"Mulder, I've been trying to reach you all day," she said. "Where have you been?"

"My apartment complex is being fumigated," Mulder said. "So I thought I'd get away for the weekend. I came up to Massachusetts."

"Visiting your mother?" Scully asked.

"No," said Mulder. "I'm just sitting and thinking."

"Uh-huh," said Scully. "Just sitting and thinking?"

Mulder sensed that she did not totally believe him.

"Just sitting and thinking," he assured her. "What are you doing?"

"Cleaning my gun," Scully said matter-of-factly. She paused to wipe her hands before she continued. "Tell me, Mulder, what are you thinking about? Anything special?"

"There were widespread accounts of unidentified colored lights hovering in the skies around here last night," Mulder admitted.

"So you're just sitting and thinking," Scully said. "And maybe giving the sky a once-over at the same time."

"Scully, I know it goes against your grain," said Mulder, "but did you ever look up at the stars and feel that something is out there? That it's looking down at you at that very moment? That it's as curious about you as you are about it?"

"Mulder, we've been through this before," Scully said with a sigh. "It was a freak chemical accident that created life on Earth. It was sheer biological luck that produced the complex intelligence that we humans possess. The odds against there being intelligent alien life-forms are as high as the sky you like to stare at. It's downright anti-Darwinian."

"Just cleaning your gun, huh?" Mulder asked, in an attempt to change the subject. He didn't feel like getting into the same old argument again. He had more star-gazing he wanted to do tonight. Even as he talked to Scully, his eyes returned to the sky, as if drawn by a magnet.

Scully let out an exasperated sigh. "Someday maybe you'll listen to reason," she said, not sounding too hopeful.

"I understand what you're saying, Scully," Mulder said. "But I still need to keep looking."

Noticing more bugs on the windshield, he turned the wipers back on.

"Just don't look too hard, Mulder," Scully advised. "You might not like what you find."

"Isn't that what Dr. Zaius said to Charlton Heston at the end of *Planet of the Apes*?" asked Mulder.

"Right," said Scully. "And look what happened."

Mulder had just opened his mouth to answer when a dazzling light seemed to explode through the windshield.

It took a moment before Mulder could speak. And then all he could blurt out was, "Scully, I have to go."

"Mulder, what is it?" Scully asked, suddenly concerned.

But all she heard was the click of his phone cutting off.

"Mulder?" she tried again. But there was no sound on the line.

Chapter THREE

Blinded by the blast of light, Mulder put down the phone and reached toward the gun in his shoulder holster.

Then he relaxed as his eyes adjusted to the glare and he saw a policeman behind the bright light of a flashlight. The wipers moved to and fro in front of the cop's narrowed eyes as he squinted in through the windshield at Mulder.

The cop moved to the open side window, keeping the light on Mulder.

"How you doing?" he asked. His voice was soft and easy. But the look he gave Mulder was hard.

"Fine, Officer," Mulder said.

The cop kept looking hard at Mulder. "What're you doing?"

"Just sitting and thinking," Mulder told him.

"Sitting and thinking and talking on the phone?" asked the cop.

"That's right, Officer," Mulder said.

"Planning some funny business?" the cop questioned. "Let's see some ID, mister."

Mulder shrugged. He handed his FBI identity card to the cop.

10

The policeman shone his light on the ID photo. Then he shone it on Mulder's face again. Then he gave the card another careful look.

Finally he said, "Special Agent Fox Mulder?"

"That's me," Mulder said.

"I'm Sheriff Vince Frass," said the cop, finally relaxing. "Sorry for the hassle," he said. "But we don't see many strangers on back roads in these parts. Especially not from the bureau. You here on a case?"

"I heard reports of several UFO sightings here last night," Mulder said. "Did you see anything?"

"Not personally," the sheriff said. "But we did receive a lot of calls. That kind of stuff always comes in waves. One kook gets a notion, and it spreads like an epidemic."

"Any more reports tonight?" Mulder asked.

"No, sir," the sheriff said. Then he scratched his head. "I didn't know the FBI kept track of that sort of thing."

"It doesn't," Mulder said.

Sheriff Frass gave the card another long look. Then he looked up Mulder.

"Excuse me for prying," Frass said, "but why are you sitting here with your wiper blades on?"

Mulder turned off the wipers. Then he said, "I was just knocking off some bugs that landed on my windshield. You sure have a lot of them around here."

At the word *bugs*, the sheriff's hand went to his holstered pistol. It was as if an alarm had gone off.

"Bugs?" Frass demanded. "You mean cockroaches?"

Mulder shrugged. "Maybe. Or maybe beetles. I'm not sure. I didn't get a good look. And I'm not really good with bugs."

Frass looked as if he was ready to ask more questions. But before he could, a radio sounded in the night. Frass swung around, and his flashlight beam showed a squad car parked a short way up the dark road.

"Back in a second," he told Mulder, and ran for his car. He moved fast for a man whose belly ballooned over his belt.

A moment later the squad car's headlights flashed on, and the motor roared to life. The car came down the road toward where Mulder was parked.

The squad car skidded to a stop alongside Mulder.

The sheriff leaned through his open side window.

"Sorry for the disturbance, sir," he said as he handed Mulder his ID. "I've got to be going now."

"What's up?" Mulder asked.

The sheriff's voice was grim. "Another roach attack."

"Another—*what*?" Mulder asked.

But the sheriff had already roared away.

Instantly Mulder started his car. Gunning the motor, he made a fast U-turn and followed the squad car.

Chapter FOUR

As he stood in the doorway of a suburban home, Mulder decided that he would find out more about these roach attacks before he called Scully.

He had trailed Sheriff Frass to the house. The sheriff did not mind seeing Mulder's car pull up behind his. In fact, he was glad to have an FBI special agent on hand.

"I'd be grateful for any help you can give me," the sheriff said. "These incidents are driving me buggy—if you'll pardon the expression."

Mulder followed the sheriff past two cops at the door. Inside they were met by a man with a pale face and twitching eyelids.

"I'm Dr. Eckerle," he said.

"You a new medical examiner?" the sheriff asked. "Where's Dr. Newton?"

"No, I'm a chemist," Dr. Eckerle said. "I'm the man who lives here. Dr. Newton is downstairs in the basement, doing tests on the corpse. I didn't want to stay down there any longer. Bugs give me the creeps to begin with. And these—*ugh*."

"Bugs?" the sheriff said sharply. "You mean cockroaches?"

14

Dr. Eckerle swallowed hard and nodded.

"Which way to the basement?" the sheriff asked.

"This way," Dr. Eckerle said, and led them to the top of the cellar stairs. "Do I have to go with you? I'd really rather not. *They're* still down there."

"They?" asked Mulder.

"The bugs," said Dr. Eckerle, shuddering. "They were crawling all over the exterminator when I came down. When they saw me, they headed for cover. But it wasn't like they were scared. More like they had had enough fun for the day. It was just hideous."

"Don't worry," said the sheriff, patting his holstered pistol. "We have enough firepower to deal with them. And we might need you to answer some questions."

Reluctantly Dr. Eckerle followed the sheriff and Mulder down the stairs.

There they found Dr. Newton, a man about forty years old with a bald head and rimless glasses. With him were two assistants conducting tests on the corpse lying on the concrete floor.

Dr. Eckerle stood as far away as possible as the sheriff and Mulder looked down at the dead man. His body showed no signs of violence, except for the look of pure terror frozen on his face.

Mulder briefly listened as the sheriff and the medical examiner discussed the case. After a few minutes, he had heard enough to take his cellular phone from his pocket.

Scully answered on the first ring.

"I think you'd better get up here," Mulder said.

"What's up?" she asked.

"It appears that cockroaches are attacking and killing people," Mulder said.

"Mulder," Scully said, "I'm not going to ask you if you just said what I think you said. Because I know it's what you said."

"Scully," Mulder said, "I'm crouched over a dead exterminator. He was discovered with cockroaches crawling all over his corpse. The local sheriff says two other bodies were found in the same condition this afternoon."

"Exactly where in Massachusetts are you?" Scully asked.

"A community called Miller's Grove," said Mulder. "It's near a large university and a couple of high-tech companies, which means it's home to a lot of scientists. The other roach attacks involved a molecular biologist and a physicist. The witness to this most recent attack is a chemist working on alternative fuel research. These reports are coming from intelligent people trained in clear-sighted observation."

Behind him, Mulder heard Dr. Eckerle telling the sheriff, "The image of those cockroaches is burned into my brain. I see them every time I close my eyes."

"Try not to close your eyes," the sheriff advised.

"But how will I sleep?" Dr. Eckerle said. "And where? I certainly can't spend the night here. In fact, I'm putting the house on the market as soon as I can—though I don't figure to sell it once the news is out."

"Better check into a motel until we solve this thing," said the sheriff.

"You really think you will?" asked Dr. Eckerle. He didn't sound convinced.

"Sure we will. That's our job," the sheriff said. He didn't sound convincing.

Meanwhile, Scully was asking over the phone, "Did the body have insect bites?"

"Insect bites?" asked Mulder, glancing at Dr. Newton.

The medical examiner firmly shook his head.

"Not a one," Mulder said to Scully.

"Mulder, millions of people are very allergic to cockroaches," Scully said. There were occasions when her medical training came in handy. This was one of them. "That allergy can be deadly."

"You mean all it takes to kill a person is simple contact with a roach?" said Mulder.

"If that person is allergic enough," Scully affirmed. "The body goes into anaphylactic shock."

"Anaphylactic shock?" Mulder repeated the unfamiliar term.

When Dr. Newton heard it, he nodded his head vigorously.

"Many such reactions occur in people who come into frequent contact with roaches," Scully said. "It dangerously increases their sensitivity. This high-risk group includes a high percentage of exterminators. I think that explains your little mystery."

"Well, I'll check it out," said Mulder, but he did not sound happy about it.

"Of course, if you disagree, I could still come up there."

"No," said Mulder, suppressing a sigh. "I'm sure you're right. Thanks, Scully. See you when I get back to D.C. Good night."

"'Night," said Scully.

Mulder clicked off the phone.

"Who was that?" the sheriff asked.

"My partner and scientific resource," said Mulder.

"Fills you in on data, huh?" the sheriff asked.

"That—and brings me back to earth," Mulder replied.

Chapter FIVE

Alice Wong was the first girl in her high school ever invited to join the Albert Steiner Science Club. True, there were only two other members—Albert and his best friend and fellow nerd, Jason Smith. True, nobody knew about the club except Albert, Jason, and now Alice. Still, Alice supposed it was a kind of honor. Anyway, it was nice to have somebody recognize that a girl could be just as much of a scientist as a boy.

Now she was being honored even more. Albert and Jason were letting her visit Albert's private laboratory. It was in Albert's house.

Alice was a little suspicious, though. Were Albert and Jason planning some kind of initiation into their club? Alice told herself to keep cool. No way these guys were going to gross her out.

"You'll be interested in my latest project," Albert said to Alice and Jason as he unlocked the attic door. His eyes gleamed behind black-rimmed glasses. The look on his face reminded Alice of Dr. Frankenstein as he prepared to bring his monster to life.

Albert swung open the door and led the way up

the stairs. Alice's eyes widened as she reached the top. The room was crammed with equipment. Alice saw microscopes, Bunsen burners, glass slides, test tubes, and jars upon jars of chemicals, not to mention ratty-looking white mice scurrying around cages.

"Cool, huh," Albert said proudly.

"Cool," Alice agreed, though she wondered how many years ago the place had last been cleaned. Clearly Albert wasn't too concerned with sterile lab conditions.

"So what are you working on now?" Jason asked. "You've been real hush-hush about it."

"I wanted to perfect my work before I revealed it to the world," Albert said.

Alice and Jason watched as Albert put chemical crystals into a test tube. Then he prepared to pour an acid solution over them.

"That stuff isn't going to explode, is it?" Alice couldn't help asking.

"Yeah, I heard about that last experiment of yours," Jason said. "My dad told your dad he had to raise your dad's insurance rates."

Albert shrugged. "No pain, no gain."

He poured the acid. It hit the crystal. Pinkish smoke rose out of the test tube. It filled the attic in minutes.

"What does it smell like?" Albert demanded.

Alice took a sniff. "Well, it's kind of sweetish, sort of like . . . like . . ."

"It smells exactly like roses," Albert announced triumphantly.

"But what's it good for?" Jason asked.

"That's not my worry," Albert said. "I'm a pure scientist, not a businessman."

"Well, I don't know about that. I think . . ." Jason began, then paused with an annoyed look.

"What's the matter?" asked Alice.

"My arm, it's started itching real bad," said Jason as he began scratching it.

"Maybe you're allergic to the smoke," Alice suggested.

"Hmm, possible allergic reaction," said Albert, grabbing a notebook and jotting down a note. "There may be some kinks to work out."

His brow furrowed as he looked down at his notebook and thought.

Then his head jerked up as Jason screamed.

Jason was looking down at his arm. "Get it off!" he cried.

Alice took a look at Jason's arm and tried to keep her stomach from turning over.

Cool it, cool it, it can't be real, it's some kind of trick, she told herself.

But she heard herself saying, "*Ughh*. I'm gonna be sick."

"Hmm," Albert said, his tone very scientific. "Interesting. Never saw anything like that. Usually they just go after breadcrumbs and stuff like that."

A large cockroach was burrowing into the flesh of Jason's forearm as Jason watched it, bug-eyed with terror.

"Don't freak out," Albert told Jason. "Try to catch it alive. We can study it."

Jason wasn't listening. Desperately he scratched at his skin, trying to pull the cockroach out. But he was too late. The roach had gotten all the way under the skin. He could see the bump it made as it slowly crawled beneath the skin up his arm.

"Aghhh," he gasped, then felt an itching on his other wrist.

"Nooooo!" he shouted as he saw another roach burrowing there.

Before his two friends could stop him, he grabbed a scalpel from a nearby table. He started slashing at the moving bump in his arm.

"Stop! You'll hurt yourself!" Alice cried, grabbing at his arm. But Jason backhanded her away and kept cutting, intent on getting the bugs out of his skin.

"Hey, man, cool it," said Albert, and hit Jason with a tackle, knocking him to the floor.

Alice leaped onto Jason's knife arm, pressing it to the floor with her full weight as he struggled to free it.

Together Albert and Alice tried to get the knife away from Jason and stop him from cutting himself to shreds.

But they were too late.

Chapter SIX

"This will get rid of you—you rotten little bugs," Scully muttered. With one hand she held the writhing victim of the bug attack.

With her other hand she held a bottle. Its label read DIE, FLEA, DIE!

"This is for your own good—you'll feel better when it's over," she told her struggling dog, Queequeg, as she kept him from leaping out of her kitchen sink. Vigorously she worked the flea shampoo into a rich lather on his fur.

Then her phone rang.

"Stay, Queequeg!" she commanded the dog as she went to the phone across the room. Out of the corner of her eye, she saw Queequeg leap out of the sink and scurry for cover. So much for the doggie discipline school she had sent him to, she thought, as she snatched up the phone. "Hello," she said.

"Scully, it's me," Mulder's voice said at the other end.

"Look, Mulder, I'm in the middle of something right now," Scully said.

"So am I," Mulder said.

"Don't tell me it's the killer cockroaches again,"

said Scully with an inward sigh. "I thought you dropped the idea."

"Scully, I've changed my mind," Mulder said. "You better get up here."

Scully grimaced. "You mean there's been another roach attack? Or I should say, you *think* there's been one?"

"I'm crouching over the lifeless body of a teenager named Jason Smith," Mulder said. "With me are the local medical examiner, Dr. Newton, and the local police. We've been questioning two other teenagers, a boy and a girl, who witnessed the death. They were slightly hysterical when we arrived, but they've calmed down enough to describe the incident. Scully, this was no allergic reaction to cockroaches. Both witnesses agree that the victim was shouting about roaches burrowing into him."

"Before we leap to conclusions, and before I jump on a plane, let's check out the facts, okay?" Scully said.

"Agreed," Mulder said.

"Are the insects still in the corpse?" Scully demanded.

"We haven't located any," Mulder admitted. "But there are wounds all over the body."

"Made by the cockroaches?" Scully asked.

"The victim did use a scalpel to try to cut the

insects out," said Mulder. "But we aren't certain that all the victim's wounds were made by the scalpel—except for the severed artery."

"You're saying that the artery was severed by the victim himself?" asked Scully.

"It would seem so," said Mulder.

"And it was the severed artery that caused the death," said Scully.

"That's the medical examiner's opinion," Mulder said. "But it doesn't rule out the possibility of a roach attack. We still have the eyewitness testimony of the victim's friends."

"Mulder, where did this incident take place?" asked Scully.

"In the attic of one of the kids' homes," Mulder said.

"And what were the three of them doing in the attic?" Scully asked.

"It seems the attic was being used as a laboratory," said Mulder. "They were working on a science project."

"What kind of science project?"

"It involved producing a chemical gas," said Mulder.

"A gas? What sort of gas?" Scully asked.

"We haven't determined its exact nature," said Mulder. "We're sending it to be analyzed."

"Mulder, certain chemicals when inhaled can produce severe mental disorders," Scully said. "One common disorder is the illusion that bugs are attacking you. The victim well may have suffered from this disorder."

"And the other kids?" Mulder continued. "They claim to have seen the bugs, too."

"They also inhaled the chemical, I presume?" Scully asked.

"They did," said Mulder. By now his answers came more slowly. Excitement was draining out of his voice.

"The mere suggestion that there were bugs could have made them see bugs as well," said Scully. "Especially if the victim of the alleged attack described it in a vivid and violent manner. This kind of hallucination is known as Ekbom's syndrome."

"Ekbom's syndrome?" said Mulder. There was a pause. Then he said, "Dr. Newton is nodding at the term. It seems he agrees with your diagnosis."

"The victims often cut themselves in an attempt to extract the imaginary insects," Scully went on.

There was a silence on the other end of the line.

Scully kept silent for a moment, then asked in her sweetest voice, "Still want me to come up?"

Mulder's voice was that of a defeated man. "No. You're probably right. Sorry to have bothered you."

"No bother, Mulder," Scully said cheerfully. "Now, if there's nothing else . . ."

"There's nothing else," said Mulder.

"Then I'll be seeing you when you get back to Washington," Scully said. "If you'll excuse me, I have things to do."

After Scully hung up, she shouted, "Queequeg, come here."

Obediently the dog trotted back into the room, his tail between his legs.

Mulder's face was glum as he put down the phone. He hated it when Scully was right about these things.

"Did you get anything else out of the witnesses?" he asked the sheriff, but without much hope in his voice.

The sheriff shook his head. "The kids are still in semishock. But even when they come out of it, I don't think they'll have much to add."

"We could test them for chemicals they may have inhaled," said Mulder dully. He could feel the trail he was on growing as cold as the body on the attic floor.

But even as the sheriff nodded in reply, Mulder came to life.

His eyes brightened, and he started to tiptoe slowly across the lab.

He saw the others watching him and held his finger to his lips.

When he reached a steel laboratory table, he slowly squatted down, careful not to make a sound. He paused for a split-second. Then his hand shot out. Bingo!

Triumphantly he held his clenched hand high in the air.

"I've caught one!" he said. "It was hanging under the tabletop. Quick, get a container!"

Sheriff Frass grabbed a small beaker and rushed it to him. The others were right behind the sheriff. They crowded around Mulder as he held his clenched hand over the opening.

Mulder opened his hand just enough for the roach to drop out. But nothing fell into the beaker. He frowned.

"I must have held it too tightly," he said. "I think I killed it."

He slowly opened his hand. Nothing was left of the roach but black, crushed bits.

"You didn't kill it," the sheriff said. "You totally annihilated it."

"It wasn't a roach after all," said Mulder. "It was just a shell. There was nothing inside. The roach must have shed it and moved on. They do that, you know."

"Tough luck," the sheriff said, seeing Mulder's disappointment. "Maybe we'll get a real roach next time. Anyway, at least we have evidence that roaches were actually here."

Mulder looked down at his palm and began to brush away the crushed bits of the roach's exoskeleton. He stopped suddenly, and excitement rose in his voice as he said, "We have more than that, Sheriff."

He held his palm out to Sheriff Frass. It was bleeding from scores of tiny cuts.

"I think that bug's shell was made out of metal," Mulder said.

Chapter **SEVEN**

"The cuts aren't serious—little more than scratches," Dr. Newton told Mulder.

The two of them were in Dr. Newton's office at the local hospital. The doctor was checking out the cuts on Mulder's hand.

"Could the scratches have been caused by bits of metal?" Mulder asked.

"Let's wait for the test results before we draw any conclusions," the doctor said. "The lab is doing a full analysis of the roach shell fragments."

"I think I know what they'll find," said Mulder, looking down at his palm. It had stopped bleeding, but the tiny cuts still stung.

"Quite possibly you're right," Dr. Newton said.

Then the doctor cleared his throat. He looked uncomfortable. "Agent Mulder, as a doctor I like to speak frankly to my patients," he said. "No matter how unpleasant the truth is, it's always best to get it out in the open."

He paused, as if reluctant to go further.

Mulder looked down at his hand. He flexed it. It didn't seem that bad. But there was no mistaking the concern in the doctor's voice.

"Don't worry, Doctor," Mulder said. "I'm not the type to panic. What do you have to tell me?"

Dr. Newton shook his head. "You don't understand," he said. "I need *you* to tell me something."

The doctor leaned forward, his gaze locking with Mulder's. "Agent Mulder, what the devil is going on around here?"

Mulder shrugged and shook his head.

"I don't know," he said. "I'm not sure. Perhaps there is something unusual going on, as certain bits of data indicate. Perhaps there's a simpler explanation, as my partner back in Washington seems to believe. There's still not enough hard evidence to go on."

The answer did not satisfy Dr. Newton. "Are we in any danger?" he asked, searching Mulder's face for a clue.

"I don't know," Mulder repeated, poker-faced.

"Should I get my family out of the area?" Dr. Newton persisted.

"I really couldn't say," Mulder said, stonewalling.

Dr. Newton was about to ask another question when the sheriff came into the office.

"Doctor, they're ready for you to examine the boy's body," Sheriff Frass said.

Dr. Newton reluctantly turned away from Mulder. The doctor put his fingertips to his forehead, right between his eyes, and rubbed hard. Then he gave his head a couple of strong shakes.

"I'll get to work in a couple of minutes," he said. "First I'm going to go to the john and splash some cold water on my face. I want to clear my mind. I feel like I'm in a fog. Everything in this case seems so murky."

After the doctor left, still shaking his head, Sheriff Frass asked Mulder, "What's Newton's problem?"

"I think he's upset that I don't know what's going on," Mulder said.

The sheriff nodded. Then he leaned toward Mulder, lowering his voice. "Between you and me, Agent Mulder, what *is* going on?"

"As I told the doctor," Mulder said patiently, "I don't know for sure. This investigation is still in the early stages. It would be irresponsible of me to cause undue concern. Nothing is more dangerous than wild rumors and unfounded fears."

"Come *on*," the sheriff urged, putting his face uncomfortably close to Mulder's. "You can tell me. I know you're with the government, and I know what it's up to around here."

"Just because I work for the federal government, that doesn't make me an expert on cockroaches," Mulder said, backing away a half step. Then it was his turn to lean forward. "Tell me, Sheriff, what *is* the government up to?"

"You're saying that you don't know about the government experiments being conducted in this area?" the sheriff asked with clear disbelief.

"Experiments?" replied Mulder. Suddenly he was all ears.

"A couple of months ago, a man from the government showed up," the sheriff said. "The guy claimed to be an agent of the Department of Agriculture. He leased a couple of acres on the edge of town. First thing he did was to put a fence up around the property. Then a building went up, large sealed crates were shipped in, and more government people arrived. They've kept what they're doing there very hush-hush. All you can be sure of is that it's top secret."

"So what do you think it is?" asked Mulder.

"You've heard about killer bees?" the sheriff asked.

"I have," Mulder acknowledged.

"Then you also know that they were a scientific experiment that went wrong—and got loose on an innocent public," said the sheriff.

"I've heard stories to that effect," Mulder admitted.

"Then what's to say the government hasn't created a new breed of killer cockroach?" asked the sheriff. "Just another foul-up. Just more innocent victims. And just maybe another cover-up."

The sheriff gave Mulder a hard, accusing look.

Before Mulder could respond, a nurse entered the room. She picked up a tray of instruments from a counter and went out again. Mulder waited until she had closed the door behind her before he answered.

"Sheriff Frass," he said, "you might want to keep your theory to yourself until we can see things more clearly. We don't want to create a panic among the people around here. The last thing we need right now is mass hysteria."

Mulder had barely gotten that last word out when the screaming began.

Chapter EIGHT

Mulder and the sheriff rushed to the source of the screaming. Their search led to a door marked MEN'S ROOM. STAFF ONLY.

A crowd of doctors, nurses, and orderlies clustered in front of it. Sheriff Frass elbowed his way through them as Mulder followed. Both men pulled out their guns.

As they entered the men's room, Mulder saw the cause of the commotion. Dr. Newton lay facedown on the tile floor. A young doctor knelt beside him, feeling for his pulse. An orderly stood nearby, pale and trembling.

"You the one who screamed?" the sheriff asked.

"Yeah, and you would have, too, if you saw what I did," the orderly said. The memory made him tremble still harder.

"Calm down," said the sheriff.

"Easy for you to say," the orderly said. But he did get a grip on himself.

"What did you see?" asked Mulder.

"I came in here and found him lying there, just like he is now," the orderly choked out. "Except that then he was covered with roaches. Lots and lots of them. Filthy little things. I hate them. No way they should have been here. Not in a hospital. But they were here, all right. They were all over him. I've never seen anything like it. I hope I never see it again."

From the look on the orderly's face, he was still seeing them.

Mulder and the sheriff swiftly scanned the room.

"I don't see any roaches," the sheriff said.

"I went out to call for help," the orderly said. "When I came back, they'd all disappeared."

Mulder was examining the men's room more closely. Remembering Dr. Newton's comment about splashing some water on his face, he headed over to the row of sinks.

His eyes narrowed, and he bent over one of the basins.

"Found one," he said, spotting a cockroach at the bottom of the basin. The bug was lying motionless on its back, its feelers in the air.

The sheriff bent to look. "Well, at least we know they can die. Wonder what killed it?"

"We can find out in the lab," Mulder said. He reached down for it.

"Gently, gently," the sheriff cautioned. "Not too tight. Remember last time."

"Right," Mulder nodded.

Carefully Mulder closed his thumb and forefinger

over the roach. Slowly he lifted it out of the basin.

He held it up for a closer look.

"It doesn't appear unusual," he said. "Just your normal, ordinary, run-of-the mill—"

That was as far as he got.

Without warning, the cockroach leaped out of his grip. It landed back in the basin. Before Mulder or the sheriff could make a move, it fled down the drain.

Sheriff Frass shook his head in disgust.

"Maybe I should handle the roaches from now on, Agent Mulder," he said.

Mulder didn't waste time answering. He reached into his jacket pocket and pulled out his cellular phone.

Scully answered on the fourth ring.

"Who died now, Mulder?" she said testily.

"The medical examiner," Mulder said. "His body was found in the hospital men's room, covered with roaches. I really think you should come up here."

"The men's room, you say?" said Scully.

"That's right," Mulder said.

"What was he doing there—or shouldn't I ask?" Scully said.

"He seemed to have a headache, from the way he was rubbing his forehead," Mulder said. "He complained of clouded vision. He thought dousing his face with cold water might help."

"Uh-huh," Scully said. "Mulder, do me a favor and check his eyes."

Mulder bent down to the corpse on the floor and did as requested.

"What am I supposed to see?" he asked.

"Is one of his eyes bloodshot—and does the pupil of that eye seem unusually large?" Scully asked.

"Which eye?" Mulder asked.

"It doesn't matter," Scully said.

Mulder pushed up the lid of one of Newton's sightless eyes, and then the other.

"Yes," Mulder said into the phone. "The left one fits that description."

"He may well have had a brain aneurysm," said Scully.

"A brain aneurysm?" asked Mulder.

Hearing the words, a young doctor in the room nodded.

Meanwhile, Mulder was listening to Scully explaining, "It has all the signs of one. An aneurysm occurs when a blood vessel bursts inside the body. It happens fast, without much warning. And when it happens in the brain, it's usually fatal."

"But what could have caused it?" Mulder asked.

"The blood vessel is usually weak to begin with," Scully said. "Any kind of strain can make it suddenly give way. Tell me, Mulder, was the medical examiner engaged in any strenuous physical activity?"

"No," Mulder said.

"Was he under any strong emotional stress?" Scully asked.

"Yes," Mulder admitted.

"Then I think we have a reasonable explanation of the cause of death," Scully said. "Now, unless you have any other questions, I'd like to get some sleep."

Mulder made one last try. "How do you explain the roaches?" he demanded.

"Did you catch any?" Scully asked.

"Yes," Mulder said. Then he bit his lip and said, "Well, almost."

"Then I don't know what to tell you," Scully said. Then she asked, "Mulder?"

"Yes?" he said.

"I hope you're not telling me that you believe you've come across an infestation of killer cock-roaches?"

"I'm not sure what to believe," Mulder said. "Would you look into it? I don't have access to the proper data bank up here."

"I'll do that," Scully said.

Chapter NINE

Mulder was not holding his breath waiting for Scully's report.

He was breathing hard as he climbed a high chain-link fence in the dead of night.

A sign on the fence said in letters impossible to miss: NO TRESPASSING—PROPERTY OF THE UNITED STATES DEPT. OF AGRICULTURE.

Squinting through the fence, Mulder had wondered what on earth it was for. All he could see on the property was an ordinary-looking house. It was the kind of house found in suburbs all across America.

Mulder reached the top of the fence and dropped to the other side. His knees bent to cushion the shock of landing. Then he moved cautiously toward the house. He had waited a half hour before making his move. But just because he hadn't seen a watchman didn't mean there wasn't one inside.

Brrrng. His cellular phone went off.

His hand shot to his pocket to grab it, click it on, and stop the noise.

"Mulder," he whispered into the mouthpiece.

"Mulder, I've been doing some research," Scully told him.

"And?"

"I have found something. Not much, but something," Scully said.

"What?" Mulder asked. It was an effort to keep his voice down. He glanced nervously at the house, but there was no sign of life.

"Back in the mid-1980s, a type of cockroach previously found only in Asia suddenly showed up in Florida," Scully said. "Since then, that particular breed has spread all over America."

"Do they attack people?" asked Mulder eagerly.

"Sorry, Mulder, but the answer is no," Scully said. "They are different from native American roaches, though. They can fly for long distances. And they are attracted to light."

"But they don't attack people," Mulder said glumly.

"Mulder, you're not following me," Scully said impatiently. "I'm suggesting that if one alien species of roach could arrive in this country, another one could, too. And *that* one *might* be attracted to people."

By now Mulder had reached the house. With the phone still at his ear, he peeked in through a window. But the room inside was dark.

"It makes perfect sense, Scully, and I don't like

it at all," he told her. "I've found out that a government agency is conducting secret experiments up here. It claims to be the Department of Agriculture, but that's far from certain. I believe it's worth investigating."

"Mulder," said Scully with a sigh. "You're not thinking of trespassing on restricted government property again, are you? I know it's paid off in the past, but it *is* highly improper activity. And I don't think that this justifies—"

"Too late," Mulder said. "I've already hopped the fence."

"Mulder, you'll never learn," Scully sighed. But she couldn't keep from asking, "So what's going on? What do you see?"

"Not much from where I'm standing," Mulder said. "There's a house on the property. I'll have to try to enter."

"Be careful," Scully said.

"Aren't I always?" asked Mulder.

"As I said, be careful."

"I'm trying the door," said Mulder. "It's locked."

"Figures," said Scully.

"I think I can get it open," Mulder said, inserting a small pick in the lock. He wiggled it until he heard a click. "Here we go," he said to Scully. "Great security they have here."

"It's so hard to get good help these days," said Scully. "Even for the government."

By now Mulder was through the open door. He switched on his flashlight.

"I'm inside," he told Scully. "The house is apparently empty."

He beamed his flashlight around the room.

"What do you see?" asked Scully.

"Just a normal, middle-class, suburban house," Mulder reported. "A large living room, nice carpeting, simple but good furniture, a fireplace—"

"When can I move in?" Scully commented.

Meanwhile, Mulder had entered the next room.

"I'm in the kitchen now," he said. "Modern appliances, moving walls—" He stopped talking and took another look.

"Moving walls?" asked Scully.

"This kitchen wall seems to be rippling—as if waves are going through the wallpaper," said Mulder, bringing his flashlight up close.

"What seems to be causing the motion?" asked Scully, her voice tense.

"I'm trying to find out," said Mulder, knocking at the wallpaper with his flashlight. "Tapping the wall seems to increase the movement."

"Mulder, be care—" Scully began.

Before she could finish her warning, Mulder cut

in, "I see a slight rip in the wallpaper. If I widen it, I'll be able to see—"

Then he said, "*Ughhhhh!*"

"Mulder! What—?" Scully's voice was charged with concern.

"Cockroaches," Mulder gasped. "They're pouring out of the opening! Ten . . . twenty . . . I can't count them . . ."

His voice trailed off as he flashed his beam on them, and they retreated. He swung his beam around the kitchen. Cockroaches were everywhere he looked. They scurried away when the light hit them. But he could see that they moved back again the moment the light swung in another direction.

"They're everywhere!" he said, his voice frantic. "I'm surrounded. I have to hold them off. Luckily they're scared of the light. If I can just . . ."

Then he groaned, "Oh, no!"

"What is it, Mulder?" Scully demanded.

"My flashlight," Mulder said. "It's gone out!"

Chapter TEN

"Mulder!" Scully shouted into the phone. "What's happening? Are you in—?"

"Gotta go," Mulder said fast.

Scully heard the click of Mulder turning off his phone.

Scully knew it was too risky to call him again. She could only wait. And wonder. And worry.

Meanwhile, Mulder had his own worries.

He stood with his dead flashlight in one hand and his phone in the other as the lights blazed on in the kitchen.

The roaches vanished in a flash.

But now Mulder had a new problem to deal with. A much bigger problem.

Well, maybe not exactly a problem, he decided, as his eyes adjusted to the light and he saw the figure in the doorway more clearly.

More like a new challenge.

An interesting new challenge, actually.

Standing in the doorway was the best-looking woman Mulder had seen in a long time. Her eyes were bright against her dark hair. Her flannel shirt, safari shorts, and hiking boots looked surprisingly attractive.

But the look on her face told Mulder that she was not nearly as impressed with him. In fact, she looked downright angry.

"What do you think you're doing here?" she demanded, her eyes blazing. "This is government property. And you are trespassing."

"I'm a federal agent," Mulder said.

The woman's eyes did not soften. "So am I."

Mulder put his phone back in his pocket. He flashed his badge.

"Agent Mulder—FBI," he said.

"Dr. Berenbaum," the woman said. "U.S. Department of Agriculture Research Service."

"Dr. Berenbaum," Mulder said. "I need to ask you a few questions."

"For instance?" the woman said.

"What's a woman like you doing in a place like this?" asked Mulder.

"What do you mean by that?" Dr. Berenbaum replied.

"I mean, didn't your mother ever tell you about roach traps?" asked Mulder.

"What's the matter, you have something against roaches?" Dr. Berenbaum demanded sharply.

"Something against them?" Mulder faltered.

"Not at all." He backtracked, trying to cover his mistake. "In fact, I'm quite interested in them."

"Really? Then come into my lab."

"Lead the way," said Mulder, noting that she had a nice smile.

Entering the lab, Mulder saw that Dr. Berenbaum clearly had a thing about bugs.

Enlarged photos of spiders hung on the wall like pinups. There were blown-up glossies of flies as well. Not to mention great big pictures of roaches. Lots and lots of huge roaches.

Mulder looked at them and forced his stomach not to turn over.

He kept his voice calm and detached as he remarked, "Your scientific work has to do with insects, I take it."

"Good guess," Dr. Berenbaum said.

"Does your work have anything to do with roaches?" Mulder asked.

"As a matter of fact, yes," Dr. Berenbaum said. "The research team that I head is currently conducting a study of them."

"For what purpose?" Mulder asked.

"We observe how they respond to changes in light, temperature, air currents, and different foods," Dr. Berenbaum said. "The more we know about their habits, the better we can figure out how to exterminate them."

"But why keep your project so secret?" Mulder asked. "You've made a lot of people around here very suspicious of your activities."

"You think we should advertise it?" said Dr. Berenbaum dryly. "We should tell the people that we've infested a house in their neighborhood with thousands of roaches?"

"Okay, point taken," Mulder said. Then he probed further. "But tell me, these cockroaches, are they a—*normal* species?"

"They're a common variety, if that's what you mean," Dr. Berenbaum said.

Mulder tried another tack.

"Have you ever come across a type of cockroach that's—*attracted* to people?" he asked.

Dr. Berenbaum shook her head firmly. "Extremely unlikely," she said. "In fact, many cockroaches actually wash themselves after being touched by a human."

"I had no idea they were so sensitive," said Mulder.

"I'm sure there's a lot you don't know about roaches," Dr. Berenbaum said.

"I'm sure, too," said Mulder. "That's why I need to have these questions answered."

"You've come to the right person," said Dr. Berenbaum.

"I can see that," said Mulder.

"And I'll be happy to help you," Dr. Berenbaum assured him. "There are so many false notions about roaches to be cleared away."

"I appreciate your cooperation. Some people have wrong ideas about FBI agents, too," Mulder said, and his eyes met hers. Her eyes were a very warm shade of brown. Actually, Mulder felt warm himself. He thought about unbuttoning his shirt collar, but forced himself back to the subject. "So I take it there's never been a case of a cockroach—*attacking* human beings?"

"Not attacking," said Dr. Berenbaum. "Of course, they often crave moisture. So there are cases of cockroaches crawling into a person's ear or nose."

"Nose?" said Mulder, grimacing, his finger going to his nostril before he could stop it.

"What's the matter?" asked Dr. Berenbaum. "The idea bother you?"

"Me? Of course not," Mulder protested, and looked around the lab for a way to change the subject.

He spotted a live bug in a tiny glass enclosure. It was mounted on top of an electric coil.

"What's this?" Mulder asked.

"It's a beetle," said Dr. Berenbaum.

"It's part of an experiment?"

"Yes—a pet project of mine," Dr. Berenbaum told

him. "An insect's shell contains chemicals that can be ignited by an electrical charge. Watch this."

She pushed a button. An electrical charge hit the bug. Blue flame blazed from its shell like a flare.

"What's that supposed to prove?" Mulder asked.

"It's my theory that UFOs are actually insect swarms," Dr. Berenbaum announced.

"Oh?" said Mulder, as if an electrical charge had shot through him.

Dr. Berenbaum saw the light in his eyes. "Are you interested in UFOs as well as insects, Agent Mulder?" she asked.

Mulder cleared his throat. "Why, yes, in a way," he said.

"Do you know much about them?" Dr. Berenbaum asked.

"Well, a little bit," Mulder said. "But I'm always willing to learn more."

"Are you familiar with the normal characteristics of a UFO sighting?" Dr. Berenbaum inquired. "The sudden appearance of a colored, glowing light in the sky? How it moves in a nonmechanical manner? How there is often a humming that interferes with radio and TV signals? And then the light's sudden disappearance?"

"I seem to recall reports to that effect," said Mulder.

"Then you should realize that all this easily could be caused by insects swarming through an electrical field," said Dr. Berenbaum.

"UFOs are really insects?" said Mulder. "That's—fascinating."

He found himself looking into her eyes again. He saw an intense light there, like a spark leaping between them.

"Everything about insects is fascinating," Dr. Berenbaum said fervently. "They're truly remarkable creatures. So beautiful—and so honest."

"Honest?" said Mulder, blinking.

"They are born, live and die, eat, sleep, and reproduce," said Dr. Berenbaum. "That's all they do, just like it's all we do. But at least insects don't kid themselves." She paused, then said, "But I hope my affection for insects does not repel you."

"Not at all," said Mulder. "I find it—refreshing."

He was about to say more when the phone in his pocket sounded.

He pulled it out. "Not now, Scully," he barked into the mouthpiece. And he clicked off without waiting for a reply.

Replacing the phone in his pocket, he turned back to Dr. Berenbaum.

"It's so good to meet someone who shares my feelings about insects," she told him.

"Yes, I've always been drawn to them," he assured her.

"So many people simply refuse to recognize their beauty," Dr. Berenbaum said, shaking her head. "They persist in calling them *bugs*, and regard them as dirty, nasty, slimy, repulsive, disgusting."

"A common delusion," Mulder agreed, shaking his head in sympathy.

"And UFOs," she said.

"You think they're a delusion, too?" said Mulder.

"No," Dr. Berenbaum said, smiling. "I mean, you're interested in them, too, just as I am."

"It's a small world," Mulder said.

"Perhaps we have other things in common, too," Dr. Berenbaum said.

"That seems quite possible," said Mulder. He looked forward to finding out.

Chapter ELEVEN

Mulder lay on the bed in his motel room. The room was dark, except for the flickering light of the TV. He wasn't really watching it, though. He was recalling his long talk with Dr. Berenbaum. Dr. Berenbaum was a very interesting woman. And Mulder felt himself getting very interested in her.

Suddenly a word sounding from the TV caught his attention.

"Cockroaches."

Mulder looked hard at the screen.

A local news show was on. A reporter stood under TV floodlights in front of the hospital.

"This is the fifth report of a dead body found covered by cockroaches," the reporter said. "So far the police refuse to say that the insects had anything to do with these deaths."

Mulder felt an itching behind his ear. His hand shot to the spot. But there was nothing there. He went back to watching the news report.

"Police also deny the rumor that the deaths were caused by the deadly Ebola virus carried by infected cockroaches," the reporter went on. "For now, the case is being handled by local authorities. But a hospital nurse did reveal that an FBI agent is on the scene."

Mulder felt something itchy on his toe. He tore off the bedcover to inspect his foot, but there was nothing there.

He looked back at the TV. It showed two men coming out of the hospital. They wore yellow protective gear from head to toe. The gear was to ward off infectious bacteria and other dangerous contaminants.

"Police are advising you not to panic if you see any cockroaches," said the reporter. "I repeat, *do not panic*. Simply notify the police—and *leave the area immediately!*"

Mulder grimaced as he switched off the TV. That reporter should have been muzzled. Scare talk like that could set off a riot.

Then Mulder stiffened.

There was an awful tickling in his nose.

His hand flew to his nose. He blew out his nostrils.

Nothing came out.

He slumped back in the bed in relief.

He lay there for a few minutes, trying to fall asleep. It was hard when the last thing he felt like doing was closing his eyes. What he most wanted to do was turn on the lights so the room was as bright as day.

Finally he gave up on sleep. He snapped on the lights and picked up the phone.

"Mulder?" Scully answered anxiously right after the first ring.

"Yes," Mulder said.

"I'm glad to hear from you," Scully said. "I was worried. I went to sleep with the phone on my pillow. Are you all right?"

"I can't sleep," said Mulder. "This case is giving new definition to the notion of things that go bump in the night."

"What happened to you at the so-called Department of Agriculture site?" asked Scully.

"The government project is on the up-and-up," Mulder said. "They're conducting a study of insect behavior. I met the person in charge, a Dr. Berenbaum."

"A bug doctor?" Scully asked.

"The term is entomologist," Mulder said reprovingly. "As you doubtless know, entomology is a highly respected branch of science."

"Right," Scully said. "The study of bugs. Anyway, this Dr. Berenbaum, did he tell you how to catch them?"

"No," said Mulder. "But she told me everything else there is to know about insects."

"She?" said Scully.

"For one thing," said Mulder, "do you know that the ancient Egyptians worshiped beetles as gods? Possibly the Pyramids were built in their honor."

"Very interesting," said Scully. She yawned into the phone. "Did you know George Washington had wooden teeth?"

"Bambi also has a theory about UFOs," Mulder went on.

"Her name is *Bambi*?" asked Scully.

"Dr. Berenbaum," said Mulder. "Her theory is—"

"Her name is *Bambi*?" repeated Scully.

"Her parents were naturalists," Mulder explained.

"She told you about her parents?" said Scully. "You must have had quite a conversation."

"Anyway, she has this theory that UFOs are really swarms of insects. I must admit, I've never come across that theory before. But she makes a very persuasive case for it."

"Mulder, don't go overboard," Scully cautioned. "Scientists can be as wrong as anyone else. They just know how to sound more convincing."

"Can I confess something to you?" Mulder asked.

"Yeah, sure," Scully said.

"There was something I couldn't bring myself to tell Bam . . . I mean, Dr. Berenbaum," said Mulder, still hesitant.

"I . . . I hate insects," he admitted.

"Mulder, many people have a fear of insects," Scully said soothingly. "It's a natural reaction to—"

"No, I don't fear them, Scully," Mulder said. "I hate them."

He paused, took a deep breath, and went on, "One day, when I was a kid, I was climbing up this tree. I noticed a leaf. It was walking toward me. Then I realized it was no leaf."

"It was a praying mantis?" asked Scully.

"Yeah," said Mulder. "I see you know your entomology."

"What happened?" asked Scully.

"I screamed," Mulder said. "But it wasn't a sissy scream. It was the scream of seeing a monster that had no business being on the same planet with me. You ever notice how the head of a praying mantis resembles an alien's head? I realized that the whole universe might be filled with such creatures—and some of them might not be so small."

"Mulder?"

"What?" Mulder answered.

"Are you sure it wasn't a sissy scream?" Scully asked.

Before he could answer, they both heard a terrible noise. "What was that?" Scully asked.

"That was no sissy scream," Mulder replied.

"And it came from somewhere in the motel."

He got out of bed and started pulling on his clothes.

"I've gotta go," he said, hanging up the phone.

Chapter TWELVE

Mulder ran out of his room and down the motel corridor. He tore around a corner—and right into a man running the other way.

Both of them fell flat on their backs.

Then they rose to face each other.

"Dr. Eckerle," Mulder said, recognizing the man in whose basement the exterminator had died. "Fancy running into you here."

"After what happened, I couldn't stay in my house," Eckerle said. "I'm renting a room here while I look for another place. My mistake. I should have cleared out of town. Maybe moved to the other side of the country."

Meanwhile, other motel guests were making their moves. As Mulder and Eckerle stood in the hallway, men, women, and children, some still in their pajamas, streamed past them, heading for the exit.

"I heard a scream," Mulder said. "Was it you?"

"No," Eckerle said. "I heard the same scream. It was from the room next door to me. I went to see if anything was wrong and—uggh." He grimaced at the memory.

"I take it you found something wrong," Mulder said.

"Wrong? Yes, I found something wrong," said Eckerle with a mirthless laugh. "I believe you'd call it wrong for a man to be lying dead in bed covered with roaches. Hideous, crawling, horrible bugs. I don't know how many. More than I could count. More than I ever wanted to see again. Now, if you'll excuse me—" He pushed past Mulder and joined the crowd fleeing the building.

Mulder did not even try to stop him. No one that terrified could be stopped very easily.

Mulder pulled out his gun and headed in the direction Eckerle and the others had come from.

He reached a door that stood open.

Inside was a brightly lit room.

From the doorway Mulder saw the dead man in the bed. He could see the look of horror frozen on the man's face.

But he could see no roaches, even after he had stepped inside and checked the room out.

He pulled out his phone and punched in a number Sheriff Frass had given him. The sheriff answered on the first ring.

"Some news?" Frass asked after Mulder had identified himself.

"Bad news," was all Mulder had to say.

"Where are you?" the sheriff asked.

"My motel—I'm the only guest still staying here," Mulder said.

"I'm on my way," Frass said.

The sheriff arrived within a half hour. At his heels was a TV news crew. As the crew set up its equipment, Mulder filled the sheriff in on Eckerle's story.

"Of course, we can't take it at face value," Mulder said. "Eckerle may have been seeing things—crawling things. The roach attack in his house disturbed him a great deal. And when he told the other guests what he thought he saw, they may have panicked." Mulder shot a sour look at the TV people. "Panic is definitely in the air right now."

"Everyone in town can't be seeing things," said Sheriff Frass. "This is the sixth case that's been reported."

"The evidence we sent out—have any lab reports come back?" Mulder asked.

"I brought them with me—I thought you might want to see them," the sheriff said. He handed Mulder a bulging folder.

"If you don't mind, I'd like to take time to look at them," Mulder said.

"Sure thing," the sheriff said. "I'll handle the media. I'm getting used to it."

When the TV reporter approached the sheriff, Frass kept a straight face as he calmly declared that the cause of the latest death was uncertain, that there was no reason to suspect anything out of the ordinary, and that the situation was under control. Meanwhile, Mulder skimmed the lab reports.

As soon as he finished, he pulled out his phone and punched up Washington.

"Mulder, what happened this time?" Scully asked as she answered the phone.

"One of the guests in my motel died," Mulder said. "He was reportedly covered with cockroaches."

"Mulder, I'm coming up there right away," Scully said.

"Scully, don't jump to conclusions," Mulder said. "I think this man simply died from a reaction to the roaches."

"Mulder, two cases of anaphylactic shock in the same day and town is very unlikely," Scully informed him. "I'm coming up."

"What I mean is I think the man had a heart attack," Mulder said. "The local press has been playing up stories of killer roaches to an alarming extent. I think this man saw some cockroaches and it scared him to death."

"Be that as it may, something strange is definitely going on," Scully insisted.

"Maybe not," Mulder said. "Your more reasonable explanations of the deaths have proved correct."

"Which ones?" asked Scully.

"All of them," said Mulder, flipping through the lab reports. "The exterminator did die of anaphylactic shock. The teenage boy did die from his own knife wounds after inhaling a dangerous chemical. The medical examiner did die from a brain aneurysm."

"Well, that's good," said Scully. "But we still can't explain why roaches were at the scenes of all those deaths."

Mulder looked at a report at the bottom of the stack. He had missed it in his first reading. "Or how their skeletal shells could be made of metal."

"Metal?" said Scully. "What on earth are you talking about?"

"Fragments of a roach shell that I found," Mulder said. "They've been analyzed as metal."

"Mulder," Scully said firmly, "I'm coming up."

Mulder shrugged. "Whatever," he said.

Chapter THIRTEEN

Mulder had a feeling Scully was already packed. Well, maybe her coming up was a good idea. Maybe she could see something he couldn't. Maybe—

Then Scully was forgotten. Mulder had spotted a rectangular brown container on the carpet under the TV stand. He had a strong hunch what it was.

He bent over for a better view, pretending to tie his shoelaces. It *was* what he thought it was: a bug trap called a Roach Motel.

Holding it up to the light, he squinted into it.

Inside the trap, a cockroach had given up the struggle to survive. It had managed to pull three legs loose from the tarlike glue coating the interior. But its other legs were stuck fast.

"I know someone who would love to meet you," Mulder said.

He put the trap in his pocket and headed out the door.

Some people would mind being roused from sleep for a close encounter with a cockroach. But Dr. Bambi Berenbaum was not one of them.

When she heard where Mulder had found it, she could barely wait to take it to her lab. Her eyes gleamed with pleasure as she held the dead roach with tweezers and examined it with a magnifying glass.

"Can you tell me what kind of cockroach it is?" Mulder asked.

"I should be able to—it's still in one piece," Dr. Berenbaum said, turning it over to look at its stomach. "This creature is in a class all its own."

"I take it that its muscular development is unusual," Mulder said.

"Well, yes—for an insect," Dr. Berenbaum said, and placed the cockroach under an electric microscope. She gave it a hard look. Her eyes widened. "But maybe not so unusual for a microprocessor."

"You're saying that this insect is some kind of mechanical device?" said Mulder.

"See for yourself." Dr. Berenbaum made room for Mulder at the microscope.

Mulder squinted into the microscope. "Sorry, but I'm not a trained scientific observer. You'll have to tell me what I'm supposed to be seeing."

"What you're seeing is not like any insect you'll ever see," Dr. Berenbaum said.

"Have you ever run into anything like this before?" Mulder asked.

"First time," Dr. Berenbaum told him.

"Have you ever seen any reports of such a mechanism?" Mulder asked.

Dr. Berenbaum thought a moment.

"I do recall some articles in science journals," she said.

"What did they say?" Mulder asked.

"They were about a researcher who's been studying artificial intelligence," said Dr. Berenbaum. "That is, the creation of computers that can actually think on their own. It seems that he's designed computerized robots that resemble and behave like insects."

"You think that's possible?" Mulder asked.

"I haven't seen these mechanical insects myself," Dr. Berenbaum said. "But in science, anything is possible unless proven otherwise. Actually, I've asked some of my colleagues about this researcher, and they say he's quite brilliant. In fact, I've been meaning to drop by his lab to talk to him."

"He works near here, then?" asked Mulder, excitement in his voice.

"Why, yes," said Dr. Berenbaum.

"How do I get to the lab?"

"It's just on the other side of town," she replied. "But I have to warn you that I've heard some funny stories about this guy."

"What kind of stories?" Mulder asked.

"Apparently this Dr. Alexander Ivanov is a bit eccentric," Dr. Berenbaum said.

"Eccentric?" asked Mulder.

"Well, more like *weird*," Dr. Berenbaum said.

"In this investigation, that comes as no surprise," Mulder said dryly.

As Mulder headed out the door with the map that Bambi drew for him, he wondered how weird weird could get.

Chapter FOURTEEN

Mulder stood in front of a low brick building on the outskirts of town. A sign on it read: MASSACHU-SETTS INSTITUTE OF ROBOTICS.

He swung open the door cautiously and stepped inside. Everything was quiet. He moved down a bare white hallway until he came to another door. He tested it. It was unlocked. He opened it and peered inside.

He saw a state-of-the-art computer workstation. He saw a lab table with an electric microscope. He also saw an old-fashioned worktable with metal working tools and a lathe. He saw electronic parts strewn on top of the table.

Stepping inside, he approached the table for a closer look. As he got nearer, he saw a sudden movement under it.

His eye caught a small, gleaming robot with two antennas zipping across the floor. Mulder started to follow it when he heard a sudden noise behind him.

He whirled around. In the doorway was a man in a wheelchair. The man had a small, shriveled body and a large, bald head. His huge hazel eyes glowed like headlights as they looked at Mulder through thick, wire-rimmed glasses.

"Dr. Ivanov?" Mulder asked.

Somewhere along the line, Dr. Ivanov must have lost the use of his vocal chords. When he spoke, his words came out of a speaker device rigged up to his throat. The device might have been the latest in high-tech wizardry, but it sounded like a cheap radio.

"Why are you scaring my robots?" Dr. Ivanov demanded as he wheeled into the room.

"Special Agent Mulder, I'm with the FBI," Mulder said, flashing his badge. "I'm investigating a case, and I believe your work has some bearing on it."

"You need not have come sneaking in here," Dr. Ivanov said, after checking out Mulder's ID. "I am always happy to cooperate with the authorities. And I am delighted to demonstrate my work."

"I believe you're doing research in artificial intelligence?" Mulder asked.

"Correct," Dr. Ivanov said. "Modesty forbids me to say I am the leading figure in the field. But I do not know of anyone close to me."

"I believe your research involves creating mechanical insects," Mulder said.

"Correct," Dr. Ivanov affirmed again.

"May I ask how these two activities are connected?" Mulder asked.

"Come, I will show you," Dr. Ivanov said.

Mulder followed as the scientist wheeled swiftly to his worktable.

"Observe my latest creation, almost finished," Dr. Ivanov said. With tweezers, he held it up in the air.

Mulder inspected it. It was a small insect-like robot made of gleaming metal. Four of its six legs were waving slowly in the air.

"Soon you will be completed, my little pet, and scamper away to join your brothers and sisters," Dr. Ivanov said fondly as he laid it gently back on the table.

Then he turned to Mulder and said, "All other researchers have tried to make robots that resemble humans," he said. "But I decided that was the wrong way to go. The human brain is too complicated. It thinks too much. Insects are another story. They don't think, they merely react."

Mulder nodded. Then he stiffened. On the floor he saw another little robot bug. It was heading for him. He moved to one side, but the bug merely shifted directions to keep coming at him.

Dr. Ivanov saw it, too, and smiled. "You see how well it works," he told Mulder. "I use insects as my models. I give my insects the simplest of computer programs. Go to light. Go away from light. Go to moving object. Go away from moving object. All they need are these reflex responses and electronic sensors to act like living things."

"So this bug is programmed to just head toward any moving object within the range of its sensors?" asked Mulder, still trying to get away from it.

"No," Dr. Ivanov said.

"Then why is it following me?" Mulder asked, moving in circles to escape it.

"It likes you," Dr. Ivanov said.

His mechanical speaker made chuckling noises as he bent over in his wheelchair and picked the bug up. He made an adjustment to it, set it down, and watched it scurry away.

Mulder made sure it had disappeared before he turned back to the doctor.

"Who is funding your research?" Mulder asked.

"I have a contract with the government," Dr. Ivanov said. "NASA."

"Space exploration?" Mulder asked. "How does your work tie into that?"

"I am producing the finest robots on Earth, and NASA wants to send robots to distant planets and even galaxies," Dr. Ivanov explained. "Robots can operate there far better than living creatures.

Indeed, in my opinion, humans will be phased out and robots will take over the future of space exploration."

Mulder leaned forward. "A very interesting idea, Doctor," he said. "I can see you've given it a lot of thought."

"A lot of thought, and a lot of effort," Dr. Ivanov agreed. His thin body seemed to puff with pride as he sat up straighter in his wheelchair. "I think you can see how well it already has paid off. I think it is fair to say that my work will go down as one of the leading scientific triumphs of the end of the twentieth century."

"I'm quite impressed," Mulder said, thinking that modesty was not Dr. Ivanov's strong suit. On the other hand, the doctor did seem to know his stuff—and it was stuff that Mulder was interested in learning about.

"For the sake of argument, if extraterrestrial life-forms actually exist—" Mulder began.

"There is no argument," Dr. Ivanov stated firmly. "They do exist."

"Okay," said Mulder. "So if we assume that these space aliens are more scientifically advanced than us, and if your ideas about space exploration are correct—"

Dr. Ivanov finished his thought for him. "Space

explorers arriving on Earth from outer space will likely be robots. Anyone who thinks that we will be invaded by living beings with big eyes and gray skin has been brain-damaged by too much bad science fiction."

"Dr. Ivanov, I think you can help me with a little problem," Mulder said.

"Always happy to help the government," said Dr. Ivanov. "I won't even charge you."

"Doctor, can you tell me what this is?" Mulder said, taking out an evidence bag. From it he took the dead bug he had found in the roach trap.

Dr. Ivanov glanced at it. "I'm really not a specialist in insects," he said. "I understand there is an excellent entomologist working on a project near here. A Dr. Berenbaum, I believe. She would be better equipped to—"

"Doctor, I am convinced that you have the expertise I need in this case," Mulder said. "If you put the specimen under a microscope, you'll see what I mean."

Dr. Ivanov shrugged and did as directed.

Mulder watched him looking into the microscope.

The doctor froze there for a long minute. Blinking, he pulled his head away. Then he bent to look again. After another, even longer minute, he slumped back in his wheelchair, his mouth gaping open, his body limp, like a man hit hard in the solar plexus.

"Dr. Ivanov, are you all right?" Mulder asked anxiously.

The doctor nodded weakly, as if he could barely move his head.

"Doctor, can you identify the specimen?" Mulder asked.

Dr. Ivanov mouthed a few words. But no sound came out of his speaker. Mulder saw that the doctor's throat no longer pressed against the sounding device.

Mulder leaned forward and said, "Sir, could you please try to—"

Dr. Ivanov gave another feeble nod. He leaned forward to make contact with the speaker.

The sound that came out was a trembling croak, but Mulder could make out the shaky words:

"This specimen—it is beyond my comprehension."

Chapter FIFTEEN

Dana Scully was normally a cautious driver. But driving up to Massachusetts, she pushed the speed limit all the way. Mulder needed help.

The closer Scully got to Miller's Grove, the faster she wanted to get there. The first thing she noticed as she crossed into Massachusetts was the traffic getting heavier. It was the middle of the night, but it looked like rush hour. It did not slow her down, though. All the cars, minivans, pickups, and slow-moving trucks were going the other way—out of the state. Her side of the highway was as empty as a graveyard.

Still, she had to stop. She needed a road map, and the only place she saw to get one was a convenience store with three gas pumps in front. Cars were lined up in front of them, honking furiously.

Scully managed to jockey her car into a spot on the far side of the parking lot.

Getting into the store was like pushing into a jammed subway car. Scully had to wedge her way through men, women, and children, clutching everything from cookies to car batteries. She had to use her elbows to avoid being shoved aside by people swarming in to buy whatever was left.

"Excuse me, do you have road maps?" she asked when she finally reached the teenage boy at the cash register. She had to shout above the madhouse din inside the store.

The boy could only nod. He was pounding the keys of the register with one hand and using the other to grab handfuls of cash. Nobody was waiting for their purchases to be bagged.

"Mind telling me where they are?" Scully asked.

But her voice was drowned out by a big, bull-like man thundering at the clerk, "Come on, sonny boy, hurry it up!"

"What is going on here?" Scully shouted into the man's ear.

The man thrust a wad of cash at the clerk even as he turned his head to answer Scully.

Scully saw sweat glistening on his face as he told her, "Lady, haven't you heard about the roaches? They're devouring people whole! Better get out while you still can!"

"Have you seen any cockroaches yourself?" Scully asked. She kept her voice calm and cool. The last thing she wanted to do was feed the frenzy around her.

"No," the man said. "But everybody knows—they're everywhere!"

As if his own words had scared him, he turned and shoved toward the door. He didn't bother waiting for his change.

A short, plump woman with a squeaky voice took his place in front of the clerk. She poured a hoard of quarters in front of him to pay for her armful of groceries.

As he counted the coins, she told Scully, "That bozo has it wrong. The roaches aren't attacking people at all."

"That's good to hear," Scully said. "I wish you'd tell the other folks that—before they go totally berserk."

"Those roaches are spreading a deadly virus!" the woman screeched. "We're all going to be covered with black, bleeding sores!"

Then the clerk nodded, and the woman gathered her purchases and scurried out of the store.

Scully could see it was up to her to calm the crowd.

Wheeling around, she flashed her badge.

"All right, listen up!" she said at the top of her voice. "I'm Agent Dana Scully from the Federal Bureau of Investigation. I'm assuring you that you are not in any danger. Everything will be okay if nobody panics. All you have to do is calm down and act sensibly." She paused a moment before turning to the clerk. "Now, where the devil are the road maps?"

Before he could answer, Scully heard a pair of voices screaming at each other.

She looked down an aisle and saw two women face to face, both flushed with rage.

"That bug spray is mine," one of them shouted, trying to grab a can from the other.

"It's the last one—and I got it first!" the second woman snarled.

"Give it to me—or I'll squash you!" the first woman threatened.

"I'll give it to you, all right," the second woman said, and shot a jet of the spray right in the first woman's face.

"Why, you—" the first woman cried, and pushed the second woman into a shelf, goods scattering onto the floor.

"Okay, now—" Scully started to say as she headed toward the two women.

But before she could reach them, a boy pointed at a bunch of small black things moving across the floor. *"Roaches!"* he yelled.

Scully had to fight to keep from being knocked over in the stampede out of the store. It took less than three minutes for everyone to evacuate the small building. Even the clerk abandoned his post.

Scully was left alone. She drew her gun and approached the things on the floor.

She breathed a sigh of relief when she realized what they were. Chocolate mints. They had spilled out of a box that had been smashed open in the scuffle.

Scully put away her gun and picked up the box. She popped one of the remaining mints into her mouth. She hadn't eaten for hours—and she had a strong hunch that when she arrived in Miller's Grove, she'd need all the energy she could get.

Chapter SIXTEEN

Mulder stopped and stared at the robot that had followed him out of Dr. Ivanov's lab. It sped past him, as if it was fleeing something.

Mulder looked back and spotted a roach. Before it could get away, Mulder bent over and scooped it up.

"Greetings from Planet Earth," he said, holding it gently between thumb and forefinger as it desperately wiggled its legs.

He looked at it. It was a marvelous piece of work, perfect in every detail. He was glad that Dr. Ivanov wasn't there to see it. It would have made him take up tiddlywinks.

As Mulder told Dr. Berenbaum when he reached her lab, "This is the best specimen yet. Only the most advanced scientific technology could have produced it. To the untrained eye, it looks exactly like an ordinary big cockroach."

Dr. Berenbaum looked up from examining it under a magnifying glass. "Actually, it is an ordinary big cockroach," she said.

"But what was it doing in Dr. Ivanov's lab?" Mulder asked.

"Doing what ordinary cockroaches do," Dr. Berenbaum said. "Scrounging for food. Hunting for heat. Getting ready to lay a few hundred eggs. Or maybe just hanging out. Cockroaches can show up anywhere and everywhere. And they're especially common in this area at this time of year. It's one of the reasons I set up my study here."

There was a sudden ringing.

Dr. Berenbaum turned toward her phone.

But Mulder already had his out of his pocket.

"Mulder," he said into the speaker.

"Mulder," Scully told him, "this town is insane."

"Where are you?" he asked.

"I'm sitting in my car in the parking lot of a store that people have cleaned out because of an invasion of bugs they haven't seen," she said. "They don't know whether they are going to be eaten alive or subjected to a horrible, lingering death. This is mass hysteria."

"They may not be completely crazy," Mulder said. "Something strange does seem to be going on here. Actually, if anyone's going crazy, it's me. If I run into any more dead ends, I'm going to flip."

"Well, I have a promising lead for you," Scully said. "I was going to wait until I saw you to fill you in, but you sound like you could use some good news."

"What is it?" Mulder asked.

"You mentioned encountering a Dr. Eckerle?" Scully asked.

"Right," said Mulder. "He witnessed the exterminator's death. And recently another suspicious death as well."

"Is he the one involved in alternative fuel research?" Scully asked.

"He is," Mulder said. "Why?"

"Then he must be the Dr. Eckerle I turned up in the computer data bank," Scully said. "The fuel that he's researching is methane gas. One of the primary sources of methane is animal waste."

"Animal waste?" Mulder said, wrinkling his nose.

"Eckerle has a license to import waste samples from outside the country—doubtless to discover which animals produce the richest variety," Scully said.

"Must be fascinating research," said Mulder. "But what does it have to do with this investigation?"

"You can check with your Dr. Bambi, but I believe that cockroaches feed on animal waste, and possibly breed in it as well. If so, some exotic foreign species may have arrived with the samples. Eckerle's research facility may have been ground zero for the strange roach population explosion."

Mulder chewed over the information a moment, then said, "Scully, imagine if an alien civilization was advanced enough to build and send artificially intelligent robots to explore Earth."

He paused long enough for Scully to say, "Okay, Mulder, I'm imagining it. Go on."

"Then don't you think they might design their robots to be powered by methane fuel, since it would be common on a planet with so many creatures producing animal waste?"

"Mulder," said Scully.

"What?" Mulder asked.

"I think you've been in this town too long," said Scully.

"Tell me, did your data bank say where Eckerle's research facility is?" Mulder asked.

Chapter SEVENTEEN

Mulder stopped the car in front of a large industrial building. Next to it and connected to it by a complex system of pipes were a number of large storage tanks. The installation looked like a cross between an oil refinery and a computer factory.

The car headlights illuminated a sign on the front door. Big letters spelled out ALT-FUELS, INC. Smaller letters underneath said: WASTE IS A TERRIBLE THING TO WASTE.

"Bambi, you stay here until I make sure it's safe," Mulder said.

"Be careful," Dr. Berenbaum cautioned. "We're still not sure what these cockroaches are capable of . . . or even if they're cockroaches."

"It's not the cockroaches I'm worried about," Mulder said. "It's the human element."

Careful not to breathe through his nose, Mulder left Dr. Berenbaum behind in the car.

He went to the front door of the building and tried it. It swung open.

Flashlight in hand, he went down a corridor lined with doors.

He opened the first door he came to and beamed his light inside. He saw a huge heap of animal waste in its center. Next to the heap of waste was a table with a computer. And crawling over the waste like kids playing King of the Mountain were countless roaches.

This had to be roach heaven, Mulder thought as he hastily shut the door. He moved on to open the next one. More waste. Another computer. And more cockroaches.

"There has to be an alternative to this alternative fuel research," he muttered to himself as he opened the next door and saw more of the same.

Finally, opening the next door, he found something worth going into. Pocketing his flashlight, he entered a large, brightly lit lab. Rows of tables were laden with scientific equipment. Lining the walls were big storage tanks labeled METHANE GAS. WARNING: HIGHLY FLAMMABLE.

Mulder examined some sealed boxes on one of the tables.

He didn't open any of them. Instead he went through folders full of papers beside the boxes. The folders were covered with numbers that meant nothing to him.

Moving to another table, he saw a box already opened. Its dried contents were heaped beside it.

And on top of the heap, a cockroach stood defiantly returning Mulder's stare.

Mulder had never imagined that a cockroach could be so huge. It made the last one he had bagged look like a midget.

He reached for it, but he never touched it.

An ear-splitting explosion froze him.

The cockroach flew into the air as the mound of waste exploded into a cloud of fragments.

As the cloud rained down on him, Mulder dove for the floor.

He knew only one thing for sure.

Cockroaches didn't pull triggers.

Chapter EIGHTEEN

Scully brought her car to a screeching stop. She had burned rubber to get to the fuel research facility. Now she got out of her car to check out the car already there.

"Yuck." She grimaced as she got a whiff of the air. But it didn't slow her as she went to the parked car.

She looked inside.

A very attractive woman in the front seat looked back at her.

Then the woman rolled down the car window.

Before the woman could open her mouth, Scully said, "Let me guess. You must be Bambi."

"Fox told me to wait out here while he checked inside," Dr. Berenbaum replied.

From inside the building came the sound of a shot.

Scully and Dr. Berenbaum exchanged glances.

"Do you want me to go inside with you?" Dr. Berenbaum asked.

"No," Scully replied as she drew her gun. "This is no place for an entomologist."

Gun in hand, Scully raced inside the building, hoping she was not already too late.

Inside the lab, Mulder hit the floor, did a body roll, and wound up under a sheltering lab table.

Drawing his gun, he peeked out cautiously.

He saw an office door at the end of the lab half open. The lettering on the door read: DR. JEFF ECKERLE, PRESIDENT & CHIEF SCIENCE OFFICER. And in the doorway stood Dr. Eckerle himself.

In Dr. Eckerle's hand was a smoking gun. But that did not worry Mulder as much as the look in Dr. Eckerle's eyes. Those eyes were as bright as the sparking fuse of a stick of dynamite.

Then Mulder noticed what was in Dr. Eckerle's other hand.

A can of bug spray.

Suddenly Dr. Eckerle whirled around. He aimed the spray can into his office and pressed the button.

Nothing came out. It was empty.

"Die, why don't you!" he yelled, and threw the can viciously at something inside his office.

Then he leveled his gun and fired in the same direction.

"Missed again," he groaned.

Mulder took the opportunity to get out from under the table, gun in hand.

"Dr. Eckerle," he said soothingly.

Dr. Eckerle turned to face him. The crazy light in his eyes was even brighter.

"They're after me!" he said. "First at my house, then at the motel. I came here to my office to get away from them. But they're following me. There are bugs—bugs everywhere."

Mulder approached warily. His gaze flicked back and forth between the madness in Dr. Eckerle's eyes and the gun in Dr. Eckerle's hand. It was a small-caliber gun. But it could do big damage.

"Dr. Eckerle," Mulder said. "You're not in any danger. These insects will not harm you."

"Hah!" Dr. Ecklerle laughed mirthlessly. "I've seen them kill two men!"

"They weren't responsible for those deaths," Mulder told him. "But they may cause ours—if you keep firing that gun in a plant loaded with methane gas."

"Don't you understand?" Dr. Eckerle said, and his voice rose like a wailing siren. *"Bugs drive me crazy!"*

Mulder could see that easily enough. But it was harder to see a way to get the demented doctor's finger off the trigger.

"Why are the roaches making those weird noises?" Dr. Eckerle asked, looking wildly around him at sounds that only he could hear.

"In Madagascar, they have roaches that hiss by blowing air through holes in their heads," Mulder suggested.

"Really?" said Dr. Eckerle, a spark of scientific interest mingling with his madness. He lowered his gun an inch. "How do you know so much about them?"

"Actually, I don't," said Mulder. "That's why we shouldn't kill the little creatures. We should capture them and study them. Now, please, put down your gun."

"Tell me something," Dr. Eckerle pleaded.

"Anything," Mulder promised.

"Have I lost my mind?" Dr. Eckerle asked.

"Not at all," Mulder assured him. "You've merely had a long week. Naturally, you're a bit tired. And your vision of reality may be, well, a trifle clouded."

"My vision? Clouded?" said Dr. Eckerle, his brow furrowing.

A sudden thought lit his face like a lightning flash. His eyes narrowed, and his gun leveled at Mulder.

"If I can't see straight, then how can I be sure you're not a roach?" he demanded.

"Dr. Eckerle," Mulder said quickly, "I assure you, I'm just as human as you are."

Mulder had barely gotten the words out when the phone in his pocket rang.

"I can hear your chirp!" Dr. Eckerle screamed. "You *are* one of them!"

After the fourth ring, Scully gave up trying to contact Mulder by phone. She put her phone back into her pocket and looked down the empty corridor. She wondered which door to try next.

It was like a bad dream, she thought, opening one door after another and finding one pile of waste and swarm of cockroaches after another.

Then she heard the shots. And as she ran in their direction, she had the feeling that the bad dream was turning into a nightmare.

Inside the lab, Mulder desperately dodged to one side and felt the bullet whiz past his ear.

Splat! He saw a hole appear in the side of a container tank. A geyser of liquid methane gas sprayed into the air.

"Dr. Ecklerle!" he screamed. "Calm down! Stop and think—"

Dr. Eckerle, however, wasn't thinking or stopping. He wasn't even seeing straight.

Eyes bulging with mad rage, he was shooting blindly.

Bang! Another bullet hit another tank. More methane spouted into the air.

Bang! Another geyser.

Mulder looked at Dr. Eckerle as the doctor lifted his gun again. Mulder could forget about appeals to reason. The only thing that would stop Dr. Eckerle was a bullet from Mulder's gun.

But shooting a man who was helplessly deranged was not Mulder's thing.

Neither, however, was dying.

"Nice talking to you, Doctor!" Mulder shouted over his shoulder as he dashed for the lab door.

He opened it and ran—right into Scully.

They picked themselves up and stared at each other.

"Mulder, what are you—?" Scully started.

"No time to explain!" Mulder said, grabbing her by the arm and pulling her toward the exit. "Scully, we gotta get out of here! This whole place could blow!"

Chapter NINETEEN

Side by side, Mulder and Scully tore back down the corridor and out the door.

Once outside, Scully slackened her pace. But Mulder kept running hard.

He ran straight to the car where Dr. Berenbaum was sitting.

"Bambi, get down!" he shouted. Then he flattened himself on the ground.

Dr. Berenbaum ducked down to the car's floorboard, while outside Scully hugged the earth near Mulder.

Bang! Bang! Bang! Bang! Bang! Bang! Bang! Bang!

A string of explosions like fireworks going off kept them all pinned down. The explosions went on and on. It was like a hundred Fourth of Julys rolled into one.

Orange, red, and yellow flames flared in the night as windows blew out, pieces of the roof flew upward, metal girders bent out of shape, and brick walls crumbled.

Then, finally, silence.

Mulder felt something land on his head, his neck,

and his hands as he lay facedown against the earth. It was like a swarm of tiny bugs settling on him.

Scully felt the same thing.

They both had the same terrible thought.

Then they stood up and looked at each other. They could see that what had rained down on them was not alive. And they could smell it.

The contents of the building had blown up into the air, then floated back to earth.

Mulder took another disgusted sniff and muttered, "Horse manure."

"Some kind of manure, anyway," Scully said, trying to brush it off.

After a minute she gave up.

"I suppose a good shower will get it off," she said. "I don't know what I'm going to tell the dry cleaner, though."

Meanwhile Mulder was staring at the ruins of the research facility. A few small fires still lit the scene. In the east, the first glow of dawn painted the clouds in the sky pink.

Mulder thought of all the roaches that had gone up in smoke. His whole case had gone up in smoke.

He felt a hand on his shoulder.

"I'm sorry," Dr. Berenbaum said. "I know how you must feel."

Then her nose wrinkled, and she backed a few feet away from him.

Before Mulder could say anything, a police siren wailed in the distance. They all turned to see a squad car approaching.

It came to a stop, and Sheriff Frass stepped out. He took a quick look at the building.

"Any casualties?" he asked Mulder.

"Dr. Eckerle was in there," Mulder said. "I don't think he got out."

"From the looks of the place, we don't figure to find his remains," the sheriff said.

"Or anything else," Mulder said. "Methane gas burns hot."

"Still, it wasn't as costly as some of the other fires last night," the sheriff said.

"There were others?" asked Scully, deciding to enter the conversation.

Sheriff Frass looked at her curiously.

"My partner, Agent Dana Scully," Mulder said. "Scully, this is Sheriff Frass. He's been on the case from the beginning."

The sheriff shook his head wearily. "Last night there were four fires. Eighteen automobile accidents. Thirteen assault and battery cases. Two store lootings. And thirty-six injuries, half of them pesticide poisonings."

"A hard day's night, I take it," Scully said.

"Thank goodness it seems to be over," the sheriff said as the rim of the sun rose orange on the horizon. Above it the sky was pale blue. "We haven't had a report about cockroaches or anything else for a couple of hours. Maybe this town has finally come to its senses. Now you two agents ought to go home and get some rest. You look pooped."

"An unfortunate choice of words, Sheriff," Scully said, still trying to brush herself off.

Meanwhile Mulder had turned toward Dr. Berenbaum, who remained a healthy distance away from him.

"Perhaps we can have breakfast and discuss certain aspects of this case," he suggested. "After I bathe and change clothes, of course."

Before she could answer, there was the sound of another vehicle.

The four of them watched a van approaching. It stopped, and a wide door dropped down on the driver's side to form a ramp. Dr. Ivanov rolled down it in his motorized wheelchair.

"Agent Mulder, they told me I could locate you here. That specimen you showed me earlier. May I examine it again?"

Mulder reached into his pocket. He pulled out the evidence bag and opened it.

His shoulders sagged. "It's completely destroyed," he said. "There are just metal fragments—no bigger than from the roach shell I found before. Still, if you want to take a look—"

Dr. Berenbaum went to look over Dr. Ivanov's shoulder as he sifted through the fragments. Her eyes glowed with interest.

"You know, many insects don't develop wings until they are about to shed their shells," she said. "Perhaps these insects, or whatever we call them, were getting ready to fly away—back to wherever they came from."

"That solves everything," Scully said, with just a touch of amusement.

"May I borrow this specimen, Agent Mulder?" Dr. Ivanov asked. "I'd like to do further study."

"I've already had similar fragments analyzed," Mulder said. "They're nothing but common metals. What do you hope to find, Doctor?"

Dr. Ivanov was too engrossed in the roach remains to answer. He looked at the fragments with intense interest.

Dr. Berenbaum, who was looking at Dr. Ivanov with a different kind of intense interest, answered for him. "His destiny."

Dr. Ivanov raised his eyes from the fragments and looked at Dr. Berenbaum with an interest that mirrored hers.

"Isn't that what Dr. Zaius said to Zira at the end of *Planet of the Apes*?" he asked her.

"It's one of my favorite movies," Dr. Berenbaum said.

"Mine, too," said Dr. Ivanov, the voice coming out of his speaker filled with enthusiasm. "I love science fiction."

They exchanged smiles as their gazes met.

"I have found *Planet of the Apes* a film worth studying in detail," Dr. Ivanov said. "Perhaps we can find a quiet spot to discuss it at length."

"I'd enjoy that very much," Dr. Berenbaum said warmly. "Besides, I'm fascinated by your work. Have you thought of programming your robots to act like social insects, like ants or bees?"

"As a matter of fact, I have," said Dr. Ivanov as he rolled away, Dr. Berenbaum at his side.

The last thing Mulder could hear of their conversation was Dr. Berenbaum saying, "Why don't you call me Bambi?"

"Quite a pair," the sheriff said, looking after them.

"Obviously a match made in heaven," Scully remarked.

Seeing the expression on her partner's face, she said, "Don't think of it as rejection, Mulder. Think of it as a victory for humankind. By the time there's another invasion of artificially intelligent, waste-eating, alien robots, maybe their grandchildren will have devised a way to save our planet."

"Scully," Mulder said. "I never thought I'd say this to you. But you smell bad."

Chapter TWENTY

It was all for the best, thought Mulder.

Scully was right. Bamb—or rather, Dr. Berenbaum—would be happy with Dr. Ivanov.

And he, Mulder, was better off living alone.

He was free to sit in his apartment, as he was doing now, and work on what mattered to him most: filling in more blanks in the X-files.

It didn't matter if it was three in the morning. There was nobody here but him to complain about lack of sleep.

And it didn't matter if he was munching one sunflower seed muffin after another. There was nobody else but him—and perhaps his cleaning lady—to complain about the crumbs.

Sunflower seeds crunching between his teeth, Mulder typed into his computer, "The development of our brain has been the biggest step forward for evolution. Big deal. While we can get a charge from the power to think, that power is easily and often overridden by our animal instincts—the ones that tell us to react, not reflect, to attack, not analyze."

Mulder took another bite of muffin as he paused

to think. Then he resumed typing. "Maybe we have gone as far as we can go. Maybe the next advance will have to be made by beings that we create. Maybe these artificial—"

Beep! the computer sounded.

"Drat," Mulder said. He tried to move the cursor, but it was frozen. He hit a few keys on the keyboard, but the computer still did not respond.

Scowling, Mulder stood up and, leaning over, gave the monitor a firm whack on one side. The screen flickered for a moment, then came back on.

He exhaled in relief as he saw his words reappear on the screen. He went back to typing, faster now: "Life-forms that we design and create will not be ruled by simple instincts for survival. Maybe they will not be simple mechanical robots but thinking, feeling beings superior to us in every way. Maybe that step forward has already been achieved on another planet. If those advanced life-forms ever visited us, would we recognize them? And wouldn't they be horrified at seeing primitive creatures like us?"

Beep!

"What the devil!" Mulder exclaimed, glaring at his frozen screen. "I knew I shouldn't have gotten this new program. They all have bugs in—"

He stopped as he spotted a sudden movement

out of the corner of his eye. He looked over and saw a large insect moving fast across the desk.

He shuddered as the bug headed straight for his sunflower seed muffin.

Mulder grabbed the nearest object at hand—a bulging file folder.

He raised it in the air.

The insect looked up from the muffin—right into Mulder's eyes.

Mulder looked back at it. He thought of the vast space of time during which this creature and its ancestors had inhabited the planet.

How could he even think of destroying this, one of nature's greatest triumphs?

He began to gently lower the file.

But insects had not survived for billions of years on Earth by being blind.

Even this slight movement was enough to alert it. It scurried across the tabletop toward safety behind the computer.

Swish! The file lashed down.

"Gotcha," Mulder said.

THE
X-FILES

X MARKS THE SPOT

A novel by Les Martin
Based on the television series created by Chris Carter
Based on the teleplay written by Chris Carter

Class of the doomed...
The FBI thinks Agent Fox Mulder is strange – or
worse. He keeps insisting that aliens are running amok
on earth. His lovely and level-headed partner, Agent
Dana Scully, is supposed to keep him in line. But that's
hard to do when they're investigating an Oregon high
school class full of corpses and the walking dead.

Yes, Mulder's theories about the class of '89 are beyond
strange. But in a world where minds are turned off like
lights, bodies blossom with otherworldly scars, and the
night explodes with blinding evil, Fox Mulder may not
be strange at all. He may just be the one with the
answers nobody's ready to hear...

ISBN 0 00 675182 2

Don't miss the other X-Files novels by Les Martin:

X-Files #2: Darkness Falls   ISBN 0 00 675183 0
X-Files #3: Tiger, Tiger   ISBN 0 00 675184 9

THE
X-FILES

DARKNESS FALLS

A novel by Les Martin
Based on the television series created by Chris Carter
Based on the teleplay written by Chris Carter

Timberrrr!

FBI agents Fox Mulder and Dana Scully are tracking
terror in the tall timber. And they've got their work cut
out for them . . .

How can men hard as nails melt away into thin air?
Is it eco-warriors trying to protect their beloved forest?
Or an unearthly evil indulging in a feeding frenzy –
every night, when the light fails?

One things is certain: Scully and Mulder need answers
– before darkness falls . . . for good.

ISBN 0 00 675183 0

Don't miss the other X-Files books:
#1 X Marks the Spot
#3 Tiger, Tiger
#4 Squeeze
#5 Humbug

LES MARTIN has written dozens of books for young readers, including the RAIDERS OF THE LOST ARK and INDIANA JONES AND THE TEMPLE OF DOOM movie storybooks, and many Young Indiana Jones middle-grade novels. He has also adapted many classic works of fiction for young readers, including THE LAST OF THE MOHICANS, EDGAR ALLAN POE'S TALES OF TERROR, and THE VAMPIRE. Mr. Martin is a resident of New York City.